P9-CNG-636

DISCARD

Peter's Picture

Valeri Gorbachev

North-South Books

New York · London

To my daughter Sasha and my son
Kostya, whose framed pictures
I have all over my walls.

Copyright © 2000 by Valeri Gorbachev
All rights reserved. No part of this book may be
reproduced or utilized in any form or by any means,
electronic or mechanical, including photocopying,
recording, or any information storage and retrieval
system, without permission in writing from the publisher.
Published in the United States by North-South Books Inc.,
New York. Published simultaneously in Great Britain,
Canada, Australia, and New Zealand in 2000 by
North-South Books, an imprint of Nord-Süd Verlag AG,
Gossau Zürich, Switzerland.
Library of Congress Cataloging-in-Publication Data
is available.
A CIP catalogue record for this book is available from
The British Library.
The art for this book was prepared with pen-and-ink
and watercolor.
Designed by Marc Cheshire
ISBN 1-55858-965-1 (trade binding)
10 9 8 7 6 5 4 3 2 1
ISBN 1-55858-966-X (library binding)
10 9 8 7 6 5 4 3 2 1
Printed in Belgium

For more information about our books,
and the authors and artists who create them,
visit our web site: http://www.northsouth.com

One day at school Peter painted a picture.

It was a picture of a big orange flower.
It was the best picture he had ever painted
and Peter was very proud.

When school was over Peter rushed
outside with his picture. He knew just
what to do with it.

On his way home
Peter stopped to see Mrs. Dog.
"Look! Look! Mrs. Dog!" he called.
"What have you got there?" said Mrs. Dog.
Peter held out his picture.
"What a beautiful flower!" said Mrs. Dog.
"Let me smell it."
"Oh, no!" said Peter. "That's not right.
But thanks anyway."

So Peter continued on his way.
Soon he saw Uncle Bear.
"Look! Look! Uncle Bear!" he called.

"Let me see what you've got," said Uncle Bear.
He studied Peter's picture.
"Why, this is a wonderful flower," he said.
"Let me give it to my bees. They're sure to want
some of the pollen."
"Oh, no!" said Peter. "That's not right!
But thanks anyway."

Disappointed, Peter continued on his way.
Next door he saw Mr. Boar.
"Look! Look! Mr. Boar!" he called.

"What's that you've got?" asked Mr. Boar.
"Why, it's a flower! And so healthy looking, too.
Here, let me put it in a vase."
"Oh, no!" said Peter. "That's not right!
But thanks anyway."

Discouraged, Peter continued on his way.
Soon he saw Mr. Mole.
"Look! Look! Mr. Mole!" he called.
"You'll have to come closer," said Mr. Mole.
"I don't see very well."

Mr. Mole cleaned his glasses and peered at
Peter's picture. "What a splendid flower!" he said.
"Why, I've never grown one as beautiful as that!
Here, let me water it for you!"
"Oh, no!" said Peter. "That's not right!
But thanks anyway."

Peter sadly trudged the rest of the way home.
"What do you have there, Peter?" asked his mother
as he climbed up the front steps.
Peter held out his picture.

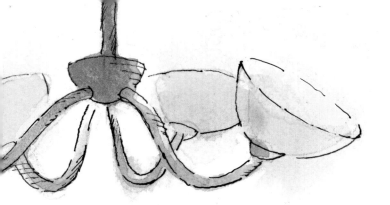

"That's wonderful!" his mother said.
She called to Peter's father,
"Look what Peter's got!"

Peter's father studied the picture.

"This is great," he said. "And I know just what to do with it."

Peter reached for the picture.

"You aren't going to smell it, are you? Or give it to the bees?

Or put it in a vase? Or water it?"

"Of course not," said his father. "What silly ideas."
He took the picture and headed down to the basement.
It seemed to Peter that he was gone a long time. . . .

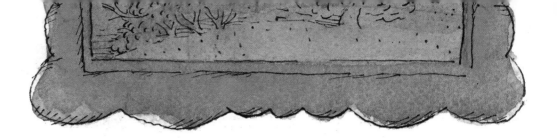

When Father returned, he carried Peter's picture
in a beautiful frame. Carefully he hung it on the wall.
Then they all stood back and admired it.
"Oh, yes!" said Peter happily. "That's just right!"
And then he hurried up to his room . . .

. . . to paint a new picture.